Tilly's Pony Tails

Goliath

the rescue horse

Tilly's Pony Tails
Goliath
the rescue horse

Pippa Funnell

Illustrated by Jennifer Miles

Orion
Children's Books

First published in Great Britain in 2011
by Orion Children's Books
This new edition published in 2013
a division of the Orion Publishing Group Ltd
Orion House
5 Upper St Martin's Lane
London WC2H 9EA
An Hachette UK Company

5 7 9 10 8 6 4

A catalogue record for this book is available from the British Library.

ISBN 978 1 440 0259 1

Printed and bound in the UK by
CPI Group (UK) Ltd, Croydon, CR0 4YY

www.orionbooks.co.uk
www.tillysponytails.co.uk

To the dedicated team at
World Horse Welfare

Hello!

When I was little, I, like Tilly, was absolutely crazy about horses and ponies. All my books, pictures and toys had something to do with my four-legged friends.

I was lucky because a great friend of my mother's lent us a little woolly pony called Pepsi. He lived in the field at my best friend's house. I loved spending as much time as possible with him, but hated having to scrape all the mud off his shaggy winter coat. I used to lie in bed at night longing for the day I'd be able to have a smart horse all clipped and snuggled up in a stable with nice warm rugs.

My birthday treat every year was to go to The Horse of the Year Show, and

I remember going to Badminton and Burghley as a child. It was seeing top riders at these famous venues that gave me the inspiration to follow my dreams.

Now I've had the opportunity to ride some wonderful horses, all of whom have a special place in my heart. It's thanks to them that I have achieved my dreams and won so many competitions at the highest level. I still ride all day, every day, live, sleep and breathe horses and I love every minute of it.

Many of you will not be as used to horses as I am, so I have tried to include some of what I have learned in these books. At the back is a glossary so you can look up any unfamiliar words.

I hope you will enjoy reading the books in my series *Tilly's Pony Tails*, as much as I have enjoyed creating a girl who, like me, follows her passions. I hope that Tilly will inspire many readers to follow their dreams.

Love

One

On Monday morning, Tilly Redbrow couldn't wait to get to school, but it wasn't school she was excited about. It was work experience week. Tilly had arranged to spend time at the World Horse Welfare head office. For a horse and pony fanatic like her, it was the perfect opportunity.

World Horse Welfare was a charity dedicated to giving abused and neglected horses a second chance in life. When Tilly heard about work experience week she knew she wanted to go and work for them. She'd sent an email asking if it was possible and they'd said 'yes'. Tilly had been looking forward to it for weeks. It was so exciting to think that it was finally happening.

Her own horse, Magic Spirit, was a rescue horse and Tilly knew that Magic was one of the lucky ones. With her help, he'd been saved from a roadside in North Cosford. He was now healthy and strong, with a glossy grey coat and large, trusting eyes. Angela thought he had the potential to be a champion. But it nearly hadn't worked out that way. Magic's life might have been very different if Tilly and Angela hadn't stepped in. It was too awful to imagine.

'Tilly?'

It was her friend, Becky. They were queuing outside the school hall, waiting for a talk from their teachers about all the things they should and shouldn't do during work experience.

'Earth to Planet Pony! Stop

daydreaming, Tilly. Time to go in,' said Becky. 'I've got a feeling this is going to be the best week of my life. Do you think my hair looks silly?' She was busy straightening her neon hair extensions. Work experience was non-uniform, so Becky was taking full advantage of that.

'It's fun,' said Tilly. 'It makes you stand out.'

'Well, that's the effect I wanted.
I mean, who knows? Maybe this is where
I'll get discovered! Oh, I'm so nervous!'

Becky was going to work at the local
radio station in North Cosford. She'd
always dreamed of being a pop star. She'd
never understood Tilly's fascination with
horses, but that didn't matter. They'd been
friends for ages.

They filed into the hall and found
their seats. There was a hum of chatter in
the air. Everyone was excited about work
experience week.

'Attention, please!' said Mr Colebrook,
the deputy head.

Eventually the hall went quiet.

'Now, I know you're all very keen to
get going to your various 'jobs', but there
are a few things we want to remind you
about before you go. First, let's talk about
manners . . .'

Tilly quickly lost concentration.
She wasn't worried about learning how to
be polite, she always tried to be anyway.

And she wasn't nervous, like Becky. She just wanted to get started. She wondered if she'd get to take part in an actual horse rescue mission. She hoped so.

When the talk was finally over, the pupils were grouped into minibuses, which would drop them off at their placements. Today they were getting a lift, but for the rest of the week they had to find their own way. For Tilly, this was going to be a challenge – it was quite a long way. She didn't mind getting up early though. She was used to it.

'Tilly Redbrow,' said Miss Leonard. 'You're on bus number 4. You're going a long way out of town. World Horse Welfare? That sounds interesting.'

Tilly smiled.

'I used to love riding when I was younger,' said Miss Leonard. 'I hope you have a good time.'

'Thanks,' said Tilly.

When everyone was aboard the bus, it set off through the streets of North

Cosford. A couple of pupils went to different shops on the high street. One was taken to the large garden centre on the edge of town. Another went to an old people's home. And the last two were taken to the local sports' centre. Then it was just Tilly left.

The bus carried on, winding through country lanes until it finally stopped in a small village that Tilly had never been to before. She looked out of the window and saw the World Horse Welfare sign. She recognised the logo straightaway – a blue and white horse's head in a circle, above green and blue writing, which said: 'World Horse Welfare, turn your passion into action.' That's exactly what she was doing. Her stomach flipped with excitement.

Two

Tilly entered the reception of the office building. For the first time, she started to feel a little nervous. She stepped forward to the welcome desk.

'Hi, my name's Tilly Redbrow. I'm doing some work experience at World Horse Welfare. Can you tell me where to go?'

'Oh, yes,' said the man. 'Laura said I was to buzz her and she'd come down to meet you. Have a seat.'

Tilly sat down on a smart grey sofa. She remembered Laura was the name of the person who'd replied to her email. She hoped she was nice. She heard the man at reception talking on the phone, then there was silence. It seemed to last forever. Her mouth felt dry and she didn't know what to do with her hands. She hadn't thought she'd be worried, but it all felt so grown up. She wondered how Becky was getting on at the radio station.

'Hi,' said a friendly voice. 'You must be Tilly. I'm Laura.'

Tilly jumped.

'Oh, hi,' she said, standing up.

'Great to meet you at last. Have you had a long journey? Would you like a drink?'

'I'm fine,' said Tilly. 'Thank you.'

She was relieved to see that Laura, with her reddish-brown long hair, looked a bit like Angela.

'Let's go straight up to the office then and I'll show you round.'

There were World Horse Welfare logos everywhere.

'Do you know much about what we do?' said Laura.

'I know you rescue horses that have been abandoned or neglected.'

'That's right. We have several recovery and rehabilitation centres throughout the UK and we aim to re-home rehabilitated horses, either as ridden or companion animals. We also do a lot of training, and

give people advice on how to look after their horses. Another part of our work is campaigning to improve laws about horse welfare around the world. And then of course there's the fundraising. The fundraising team organises all of our events and activities. I'll make sure you get to spend some time with them.'

They went through the doors. There were several offices off a main corridor and lots of people looking busy. As they passed one of the offices Tilly noticed a pile of flyers and rolled up World Horse Welfare posters lying on a desk.

'That's where Ellie and Izzy work. They're the fundraising and events team I was telling you about. They're getting

things ready for our stall at Badminton next week.'

'You're going to Badminton?' said Tilly, wide-eyed.

'We go every year. It's one of our key awareness-raising opportunities. Have you ever been?'

'No, but I'd love to.'

Laura smiled.

'So, this is where it all happens. Let me tell you who everyone is. We've got our education team in there.'

She gestured to the open door of another office. A group of people looked up and gave Tilly a wave.

'Then on the other side is our international team. Hey, guys, this is Tilly. She's here for work experience.'

'Hi, Tilly,' came a chorus of voices.

Tilly smiled at them. There were so many people, she was worried she wouldn't remember who they all were or what they did.

'Perhaps the people you'd be most interested to meet are our team of field officers. They're my team. We're the ones who actually go out and investigate concerns about horses.'

'Wow,' said Tilly. 'Do you think I'll be able to come out with you while I'm here?'

'Hmm,' said Laura. 'Some of the rescue missions we're involved in can be risky. I'm not sure your school or your parents would appreciate it if we put you in any danger. But look, if the right opportunity comes up, we'll see.'

Tilly crossed her fingers.

They walked down the corridor to the last office on the left. As they stepped inside, Laura introduced everyone. There was Alex, who manned the Welfare Hotline and took calls from the public about troubled horses. Debs and Tim, along with Laura, were the field officers on duty that day.

'Tilly's really keen to help out,' said Laura.

'Okay,' said Tim. 'If we get a call and it's safe for you to join us, we'll let you know. Do you spend much time with horses?'

'As much as I can,' said Tilly. 'It's all I've ever wanted to do. My own horse is a rescue horse. His name's Magic Spirit, Magic for short.'

'That's good to hear. Sometimes people are wary when they hear the word 'rescue', but with the right rehabilitation and support, these horses can be wonderful, giving animals. When they come to our centres, some just need a bit of TLC and a good feeding. Others need more specialist treatment. But ultimately, we want them re-homed and enjoying life.'

'Magic is an amazing horse,' said Tilly. 'I'm so glad he got a second chance. Occasionally he gets a bit spooked by things, but really he's the loveliest horse in the world.'

'Well, I think Tilly will be an asset to our team,' said Debs. 'Sounds like she knows what she's doing already!'

'Hang on,' said Alex, picking up the phone. 'I've got another call coming in – same area code as Crickle Farm. Hello? World Horse Welfare. Can I help?'

Debs, Tim and Laura glanced at each other. Tilly felt butterflies in her stomach. She hoped it would be a call that she could get involved with.

Three

'We've had several calls about Crickle Farm over the past week,' explained Laura. 'It's a run-down place out in the country, owned by an elderly man who likes to keep himself to himself. We've been monitoring the farm closely and we've given the man some guidance and advice on how to care for horses, but it's beginning to sound as though more drastic action is needed.'

'This call was from a hiker who'd seen an emaciated horse loose in a field,' said Alex.

Tilly winced.

'What will you do?' she asked.

'Well,' said Tim. 'Laura and I will drive down and take a look. If necessary we'll remove the horse and transport it to one of our rehab centres.'

Tilly looked at Laura.

'I'd really like to help,' she said. 'Please.'

Laura looked at Tim, who was already packing up their stuff.

'I don't see why not,' he said. 'We know the place and the owner. As long as Tilly listens and follows all our instructions, it should be fine.'

'I will. I will,' said Tilly eagerly.

'Let's go then.'

The drive to Crickle Farm took nearly forty minutes. Tilly sat in the seat between Laura and Tim, nervously twiddling her horsehair bracelets. Her bracelets always reassured her. One was made from Magic's tail-hairs and the other she'd had since birth. It matched the bracelet her brother, Brook, wore. Their birth mum had given one to each of them before she'd died.

Brook was a horse lover too. He'd be so proud if he knew Tilly was on a rescue mission with the World Horse Welfare team. She couldn't wait to tell him all about it. But at the same time, she dreaded the thought of seeing a suffering horse. She tried to remember that Magic had once been thin and neglected – and now he was healthy and happy. There was always hope.

Laura told Tilly stories of other horses World Horse Welfare had rescued. There was Che, a grey gelding, who'd been beaten by his owner. When they'd found him, he'd had huge sores across his back and severe emotional problems. Now he was doing well as a companion horse on a small farm. She also told Tilly about Traveller, a chestnut foal, whose owner simply hadn't wanted her. Traveller had been left to fend for herself and nearly hadn't survived. But thanks to the rescue team she had grown up safely and was a local riding school pony.

Although she was glad about the happy endings, Tilly was shocked too. She couldn't understand why people would be so cruel and unkind to their animals.

'It's awful,' she said.

'I know,' said Laura. 'I can't believe people are like that. But some of the cases we deal with are just because of the owner's ignorance. There are people who might decide to keep a horse, but don't find out anything about horse care and management – which is why our advice line and education programmes are so important.'

Eventually they came to a narrow farm track. The World Horse Welfare trailer barely fitted between its steep banks of overgrown brambles. As the path twisted and turned, Tilly could hear the branches and thorns scraping along the side.

'That'll be a new paint job,' muttered Tim.

Finally the track widened and a cluster of run-down farm buildings appeared in front of them. Tilly could see straightaway that it wasn't a safe place to keep a horse. There were hazards everywhere – rusting farm equipment, old tyres, broken glass, just lying on the ground. All of the gates were open and some were hanging off their hinges.

'This isn't good,' said Laura, looking worried. 'You two go and see where this horse is and I'll check if anyone's home.'

'Okay,' said Tim. 'Tilly, stick with me.'

Tilly nodded and followed him. Although it was a warm spring day she felt a cool shiver down her spine.

'It's okay to be anxious,' said Tim reassuringly. 'It's never nice to see neglected animals.'

'Thanks,' said Tilly.

They walked round the back of a half-collapsed barn, treading carefully because there were stinging nettles everywhere. It didn't seem possible to Tilly that anyone could live in such a horrible place, and it didn't seem fair that a horse was made to either.

Three

Behind the barn, there was a small field. It had barely a scrap of grass to munch on and looked very different from the pastures at Silver Shoe, which were always lush and green. There was no sign of a horse anywhere.

'That's strange,' said Tim, swiping a fly that was buzzing round his head. 'I thought we'd find him out here. That's what the phone call said.'

'Maybe he's hiding,' said Tilly.

'Maybe,' said Tim. He marched towards the edge of the fence and walked its perimeter. There were several places where fence posts had come loose.

'I guess he could have wandered off,' Tim called back. 'But there's a whole load of barbed wire. I'm sure that would have put him off going far. Uh oh.'

'What is it?' said Tilly.

'Ragwort. See that yellow plant growing over there? It always worries me when I see that and I know there are hungry horses about. It's poisonous to them and usually they won't touch it. Unless, of course, they're starving.'

Now Tilly felt sick with worry.

She searched for signs of the horse's presence. Laura came over to them, shaking her head.

'No one's home. There's a leak in the roof and the whole place stinks of decay. Any sign of our horse?'

'Not yet,' said Tim.

Just then, Tilly thought she heard something.

'Listen!' she whispered. 'From the barn there, I heard a shuffling sound.'

They crept over. This barn, like the other one, was very dilapidated. The roof had caved in, and ivy was growing through the slate tiles. It didn't seem likely that a horse could have found its way inside. The sound came again – a shuffling of hooves. And from the darkness, a faint, feeble whinny.

Four

'No sudden moves, Tilly,' said Tim.
'We need to approach carefully. We don't
want to alarm the horse. You wait here
while we take a look.'

'Okay,' said Tilly, remembering she'd
promised to do whatever they asked. She
sat down on a nearby tyre.

Although she understood why Tim
and Laura were asking her to keep out of
the way, she wished she could be more
involved. She couldn't explain it, but

she had a feeling she'd be able to help –
she'd had the same feeling with Magic
Spirit. There had been others too. Red
Admiral the racehorse, whose leg she'd
helped soothe. Brook's horse, Solo, who'd
been worried about a bottle in the water
jump. She'd even understood her friend
Cynthia's pony, Parkview Pickle, who had
misbehaved when his training and feeding
regime became too much for him.

Helping horses came to Tilly
instinctively, so it was hard to sit back
as Tim and Laura worked. She watched
as Tim went inside the barn. There
was lots of neighing and stumbling, but
it wasn't a very fearsome sound. Tilly
guessed the horse was too weak to get
really worked up.

Tim came out scratching his head.
He and Laura talked about equipment they
might need. When they went back to the
trailer to collect some things, Tilly saw her
opportunity. She knew it was a risk and
that she was breaking her promise to Laura

and the team, but she couldn't stop herself.
Nothing else mattered. In her mind, she
pictured what she'd find inside the barn –
a small, scrawny pony with a bony frame
and a scraggy coat, cowering in the corner.

She went to the door and peered inside.
At first she saw only darkness, but as her
eyes adjusted, she managed to make out
the curve of a hindquarter. It was larger
than she'd expected. She blinked and
followed the top line with her eyes. She
found her way to the withers, the neck
and head, then down the shoulders and
legs to the hooves. This was no pony!

'Oh!' she sighed. 'Look at you! You're
so thin!'

It was a distressing sight. The horse's
frame seemed to fill the barn – he was
huge! – but his ribs were poking out and
the ridges of his spine were clearly visible.
His mane was matted and his face was
gaunt. When he heard Tilly's voice he
looked up. He didn't shuffle and whinny.
He just stared.

'Let me see,' she whispered. 'You must be over 18hh. Is that right? I'm usually pretty good at guessing. Do you mind if I come in?'

The horse pricked his ears and side-stepped as though he was making space for

her. There wasn't a lot of room. Several of the roof beams had fallen in and were blocking the way. Tilly carefully tiptoed over, making sure she was always at a side angle. She knew that an approach from the front could be intimidating.

She made a low, quiet humming sound and held out her hand. Gradually, the horse stepped closer and began to sniff her outstretched arm. He was immediately interested in her horsehair bracelets.

'You like those, do you?' said Tilly gently. 'They're very special. This one came from my mum. She got it from the Native American tribe she was staying with – at least, I think she did. Brook, that's my brother, and I, are trying to find out more about our mum. I'm Tilly, by the way. And out there are Tim and Laura from World Horse Welfare. We're here to help you.'

The horse looked at her as though he was listening, taking everything in. The air in the barn was still and she could see why he'd taken refuge here, but she knew she had to coax him out. It wasn't safe with all those broken beams and roof tiles, and Tim and Laura needed to assess his condition.

'I know you're a bit scared,' she whispered. 'But maybe you'd like to come outside? It's a nice warm day. We could get you some water and a little food.'

Tilly stepped towards the door but the horse remained where he was. In the distance she could hear Tim and Laura calling her. They sounded concerned, but she knew she had to stay focused on what she was doing.

'Here,' she said, holding up her hand once more and showing him the bracelets.

The horse took a step forward. As he did, Tilly stepped back. She did this again, until eventually the horse followed her all the way into the sunlight.

'Good boy!' she said.

'Tilly!'

The horse twitched at the sound of Laura's voice, but Tilly managed to reassure him. When Laura saw what was

going on and realised everything was okay,
she looked relieved.

'We told you to stay where you were,'
said Tim. He sounded a bit cross.

'I know,' said Tilly. 'I'm sorry. I just . . .
I wanted to help. He's all right though.
He's being really calm.'

'He was very skittish with me,' said Tim.
'I thought we'd have a job catching him.'

'He didn't need catching,' said Tilly.
'He just followed me out.'

Laura couldn't stop smiling.

'I don't know what you did in there, Tilly, but it's worked. I think you can be an honorary member of the field rescue team for today – even if you don't listen to your instructions!'

Tilly blushed.

'What happens now?' she asked.

'The first thing we do when we rescue a horse,' said Tim, 'is give them a name.'

He reached up and patted the horse's shoulder.

'What do you reckon, big boy? What name would suit you?'

'I think we should call him Goliath,' said Tilly. 'He's huge!'

'Perfect,' said Laura. 'Goliath it is.'

Five

Laura and Tim gave Goliath a bucket
of feed and some fresh water. He ate
everything and it was clear he was hungry.
His eyes were sunken. His
skewbald coat was patchy
and dull. It was horrible
to see such a big horse
looking so weak.

'At least that should
give him some strength for the journey,'
said Laura. 'Our next challenge is to load

him into the trailer. We have no idea whether he's been in one before and it could be a frightening process for him.'

'Have you ever helped load a horse into a trailer before, Tilly?' said Tim.

'Hundreds of times,' she replied confidently.

'What we've got to remember is that if Goliath refuses, he's not necessarily being defiant, he's probably nervous. So we have to take our time and be really patient. The main goal isn't to get him straight into the trailer, but to show him there's nothing to fear in there.'

Tilly nodded. She understood completely. When she'd first approached Goliath, she'd known it was more important to make friends and build his trust than to get him out of the barn. As soon as he'd felt comfortable with her, he'd followed her out anyway.

Laura drove the trailer closer while Tim carefully slipped a halter over Goliath's head. Tilly stood at the side,

42

reassuring Goliath and telling him he was
safe. Goliath wasn't at all head shy with
the halter.

'He's an old draught horse,' explained
Tim. 'He's probably used to wearing one
of these. I expect he did a lot of work in his

heyday. Look at his white feathery fetlocks
– they're a bit dirty now, but with a good
wash and some careful feeding, he'll look
magnificent.'

'Where will you take him?'

'To a rehab centre not far from here.
They'll give him a thorough health check
and get some more food and fluids into
him. Don't worry, boy, you'll be treated
like a king!'

Goliath hung his head low. Despite the
difficult time he'd had, it was clear he was
a calm, dignified horse. Tilly couldn't wait
to see what he was like when his strength
was restored.

When Goliath saw the trailer approach,
he stepped back.

'Let's give him time to get used to
it before we try to coax him any closer,'
suggested Tim.

Laura lowered the ramp. She opened
the side ramp as well as the rear ramp.
It's so Goliath knows there's an exit and
can see some daylight,' she explained.

Laura had also removed the centre partition, so there was plenty of room.

Tim gently tugged the lead rope that was clipped to Goliath's halter. Goliath took a few steps forward. He was willing to go right up to the trailer, but he wasn't ready to go up the ramp yet. He jerked a little.

'That's fine,' said Tim. He looked at Tilly. 'We have to make him feel like he wants to go aboard, rather than being made to. Some owners think getting a horse into a trailer should be a battle of wills. That's fine if a horse is just defiant, but if he's nervous, as many of the ones we rescue are, forcing him is the worst thing we could do.'

'I've got an idea,' said Tilly. 'Goliath seemed really interested in my horsehair bracelets. That's how I helped coax him out of the barn. Maybe I could show them to him again and encourage him up the ramp? I think he trusts me now.'

'Unusual,' said Laura. 'But worth a try. He certainly responded to you before.

What bracelets are you talking about?'

'They're plaits of horsehair. I make them from the tail-hairs of the horses I meet. The original one is Native American. It was given to me by my birth mum and I've worn it all my life. For some reason, horses are always drawn to them.'

'Or maybe it's you they're drawn to,' said Tim.

As soon as Tilly approached Goliath, he pricked his ears. She held out her hand, shook her bracelets, and talked to him in the same gentle, friendly voice she'd used before. The response was instant. Goliath stepped towards her and, little by little, he made his way up the ramp. Tilly didn't even need to hold his lead rope or halter. He was perfectly happy to follow her and didn't seem bothered by the enclosed space of the trailer. As a reward she fumbled for the packet of mints she often kept in her pocket for Magic. But unlike Magic, Goliath had no idea what they were, and he spat the treat out instantly.

'Oh dear. I'll just have to stroke you instead then, won't I?' she said, smoothing his nose and letting him sniff her horsehair bracelets. 'You're very brave. Maybe I'll make a bracelet out of your tail-hairs too. Would you like that?'

Tilly tickled between Goliath's ears. She thought it was a good job he didn't have the strength to lift his head – he was so big he would hardly have fitted in the trailer! They stood together quietly for a while, until they heard Tim's voice.

'You okay in there?'

'Fine.'

'Right, let's make sure Goliath is secure, then get on our way to the rehab centre.'

The centre was a large farm in the middle of the countryside. While Tim helped get Goliath settled and sorted out the paperwork, Laura gave Tilly a tour.

'There are four centres across the country,' she explained. 'This one can house up to a hundred and twenty horses at a time. At the moment we've got about eighty here. The stable block is enormous and we've got acres of land.'

There were horses everywhere. There was lots of pasture and it was dotted with grazing horses of all shapes, colours and sizes. In between the paddocks were walkways, so it was easy to get around.

'They encourage visitors,' said Laura. 'There's a coffee shop here and they run lots of events. They even do children's parties!'

'I would've loved having a party here when I was little,' said Tilly. 'In fact, I'd still like it now!'

She and Laura laughed.

'Ah, here's one of my old friends, Jeremy Blue,' said Laura.

She leaned up against the fence and a large bay marched towards her.

'He was one of the first horses I helped rescue. He was in a terrible state, left in a cramped stables with eight other horses. When we got to them they hadn't been properly fed or looked after for months – eventually the owner was taken to court and banned from keeping horses for life. Sadly, two of them were so weak they didn't survive, but all the others have done well and are now in new homes.

Jeremy here is so loveable that rather than re-home him, the centre decided to keep him on so he could nanny some of the younger horses. They all adore him.'

Jeremy Blue placed his head on Laura's shoulder. The affection between them was obvious. Tilly smiled. It made her think of Magic.

'They never forget,' said Laura, 'that friendly face that takes them to safety.'

Six

The rest of Tilly's work experience week at World Horse Welfare was much quieter, but still very enjoyable. She had to get up early in order to make the bus on time, but it was worth it. Her mum did the journey with her the first time, then she had to do it on her own. Unfortunately, the early starts meant there wasn't time to get to Silver Shoe first thing, but Mia and Angela were happy to help look after Magic.

At the end of the day Tilly always rushed back so that she could spend as much time with Magic as possible. She could tell he was missing her from the way he galloped over when she met him at the fence. She gave him lots of cuddles to reassure him and every evening, she took him out for a long hack. She also told him all about what she was up to.

'I'm having a great time with World Horse Welfare. I helped rescue a lovely horse. They let me name him. I suggested Goliath because he's so enormous, well, he will be, once he gets his weight up. You'd like him, Magic, I know you would.'

Magic shuffled his front hooves and shook his head.

'Don't worry. It's only for a few more days,' she said. 'Then I'll be all yours again!'

Tilly spent a bit of time with each department at World Horse Welfare. She particularly liked working with the girls from the fundraising and events team, who were organising their stall for Badminton. Every day she saw Tim and Laura in the office. They always stopped to chat, and whenever they had updates on Goliath's progress, they let her know.

According to Laura, the vet and the farrier at the rehab centre were both pleased with his condition and he'd taken to the feeding programme really well.

'He's sharing a field with two other horses,' Laura explained. 'The staff say he's really sociable.'

'Do you think I could go and visit him?' asked Tilly.

'Sure,' said Laura. 'I bet he'd love to see you again.'

On the Saturday after her work experience finished, Tilly couldn't wait to spend the morning with Magic. The first thing she did, after showering him with kisses, was give him a thorough groom. Mia had done a good job taking care of him in the week, but Tilly wanted to give him some special attention.

'I've missed our mornings together, boy!' she said, as she ran a body brush over his coat.

Magic lowered his head and gave a contented nicker. Tilly combed his mane and tail and cleaned his hooves with a hoof pick. She checked his legs for signs of injury, then carefully wiped his face and eyes with a damp sponge. She knew exactly what he liked and didn't like when it came to grooming.

To both of them, it was more than simply looking after his health and appearance. It was a chance to bond, to be close to one another.

The following weekend, Tilly's mum agreed to drive Tilly and her friends, Mia and Cally, and her brother, Brook, over to the rehab centre to visit Goliath. It was a bit of a squeeze in the car but they chatted away for the entire journey. There was lots of catching up to do.

'Sounds like you were kept busy on your work experience,' said Brook.

'It was amazing,' said Tilly. 'You'll love Goliath – he's a gentle giant. And it felt so good to be doing something to help neglected horses. How's your riding been going?'

'Well, I've got the junior selection trials coming up. My instructor thinks I should be able to impress the selectors there if Solo behaves. I hope so. He's in good shape.'

He showed her a picture on his phone. Solo looked fitter than ever. He always looked good, but Tilly noticed he had built up more muscle around his neck.

'Have either of you heard anything from Chief Four Paws?' asked Cally.

Chief Four Paws was the leader of a Native American tribe that Tilly and Brook had been in contact with. They'd discovered the horsehair bracelets their birth mum had given them were similar to ones worn by the tribe members.

'I emailed him a while ago,' said Brook. 'But I haven't had a reply yet. Although he did say he'd be busy getting ready for the tribe's annual summer solstice festival. You should tell him about Goliath and the rescue mission. He'd like to hear about that.'

'I will. As soon as I get the chance,' said Tilly. 'My number one priority is to spend some quality time with Magic.'

'It really is,' said Mia. 'He missed you like crazy when you were on work experience. Angela and I just couldn't compare. When Duncan tried exercising him he was really unsettled.'

'I think we need to turn here,' said Tilly's mum, pointing to a lane on the left.

'Yes, I think I recognise this road,' said Tilly.

It was another ten minute drive before they saw the gates of the World Horse Welfare rehab centre and the beautiful stone farm house. The sun was shining and the surrounding pasture was bathed in a golden glow.

'It's a beautiful place,' said Mia.

'And so peaceful,' said Tilly. 'No wonder horses love it.'

They went through the gates and found the car park.

'I'll go and find out where Goliath is,' said Tilly. 'I'll be back in a minute.'

It wasn't long before she came across a

girl wearing a World Horse Welfare fleece. The girl stopped and smiled.

'Hi,' she said. 'Can I help?'

'Hi, my name's Tilly Redbrow. I've come to see the shire horse called Goliath. Is he around?'

'So you're Tilly! I've heard all about
you. Tim and Laura said you did a fantastic
job helping them get Goliath out of that
barn. Really pleased to meet you. My
name's Rachel. And yes, you can see
Goliath. He's doing brilliantly. I'll show
you where to go.'

'Is it all right if my friends come too?'

Rachel glanced round and saw Tilly's mum, Brook, Mia and Cally standing at the car.

'You've brought a gang! Well, I don't blame you. It's such a nice day for an outing. Goliath is in the first field on the left. You won't have any problem spotting him. Just look for the enormous one!'

'Thanks,' said Tilly.

She waved everyone over, and together they headed for Goliath's field. The others chatted, but Tilly was in her own little world. She crossed her fingers and held tight to her horsehair bracelets. Everyone had told her how well Goliath was doing, but she couldn't be certain until she saw for herself. She remembered how thin and weak he'd looked when she'd found him in the barn. She hoped she'd see a big difference today.

Seven

In the field there were three horses –
a small bay, a chestnut with a white star
and snip, and Goliath, who towered above
the other two. Tilly could tell from a
distance that he'd gained weight. His ribs
were no longer visible and his hind quarters
had proper bulk.

'He looks so much better,' she sighed.
Her stomach flipped with joy.

As soon as Goliath saw Tilly at the
fence he walked over. He came straight

towards her and nuzzled her outstretched hands.

'He obviously remembers you,' said Brook.

'Looks like he's after your fingers,' said Mia.

'It's my horsehair bracelets he wants,' said Tilly. 'He liked them when we met too.'

The others took turns to pet him for a while, but he kept going back to Tilly. After seeing him in such a terrible state, Tilly was amazed at how quickly he had recovered in just a few weeks.

There was still a way to go, of course. Goliath's coat hadn't cleared up fully and he needed to put on more weight, but Tilly could see now what a strong, powerful horse he was. It wasn't hard to imagine him pulling a heavy wagon or a traveller's caravan. His colouring reminded her of the huge drum horses she'd seen on television in the Household Cavalry parades.

'All the horses are happy today,' said Rachel with a smile. 'They like the good weather. I've just done my rounds, giving out water and feed.'

'You must be busy,' said Brook.

'Constantly. But I wouldn't change jobs for the world. I love it here. Anyway, Goliath's doing great. As you can see, he's got a lovely character. Occasionally he gets a little nervous, but that's to be expected.

Generally, despite his ordeal, he's calm and even-tempered.'

'How long will he be here for?' asked Cally.

'Oh, we're thinking another six weeks or so. He's done well on hay and we're starting to introduce feed. It takes time and patience to get a horse back to its normal weight. It can't be rushed. But he'll be fine. Some of the horses that come to us have lost up to thirty per cent of their body weight, and they still recover. They're the ultimate survivors!'

'What will happen to him when he's back to full health?' asked Brook.

'Well, we're a rehab centre rather than a sanctuary, so our aim is to re-home all of our rehabilitated horses. We have a fantastic loan scheme, where horses go to approved homes. Goliath is so good-natured that it should be easy. But on the other hand, it can be difficult to find a home for a horse this big.'

As Rachel spoke, Goliath rested his

head on Tilly's shoulder.

'Hello there,' she whispered, stroking his nose. 'You are good-natured. Make sure you eat well and keep putting on weight. We've got to go soon, back to Silver Shoe Farm, but I'll come and see you again if I can.'

Goliath closed his eyes, as though he was concentrating on the sound of Tilly's voice. Tilly stood perfectly still. She could feel the soothing warmth of his breath on her neck. It made her feel peaceful and happy.

As they were leaving, Rachel called Tilly aside.

'I wanted to tell you,' she said. 'I can't explain it exactly, but, well, I saw the way Goliath was with you. I see so many horse-lovers and volunteers come through these gates. They come and go, and every now and then I meet someone who has that special connection with them. It's a gift. And I think you've got it.'

Tilly smiled.

'Use it,' said Rachel. 'Horses need people like you.'

With Rachel's comment in her mind, Tilly caught up with the others. It had been a nice outing, she thought, as everyone climbed into the car. What could be better than seeing a rescue horse recovering and being told you had a special gift?

As they drove away, Tilly's mobile rang. It was Laura's number. She answered it straightaway.

'Tilly? Hi. How are you?'

'Fine. We've just been to see Goliath at the rehab centre. He's doing really well.'

'Ah, lovely. It's so nice of you to go all that way. Listen, sorry to call at the weekend, and I know your work experience officially finished last week, but I was wondering if you could help me out?'

'Um, I'll try,' said Tilly.

'One of our volunteers has fallen sick and won't be able to help at the World Horse Welfare stand at Badminton tomorrow. We desperately need another person and I wondered if you'd like the opportunity. It's cross-country day. They're holding it on Sunday this year.'

Tilly's jaw dropped.

'Badminton? Cross-country day? Are you serious?'

'Absolutely.'

'I'd LOVE to!'

'Great. Well, check with your parents first.'

Tilly looked at her mum, who nodded.

'It's fine,' she said.

'If you can get to the office in the morning, we'll all go together in the minibus. I'll be there, and you know the girls from the events team. They'll be so pleased you're coming. They said you were really helpful.'

Tilly beamed. She was delighted. When she'd finished her phone conversation, she looked round at her friends.

'I – I'm going to Badminton. Tomorrow.'

'Wow!' said Cally. 'Brilliant!'

'Huh,' said Mia. 'Some people have all the luck. That's amazing.'

'Maybe it's your reward for helping Goliath,' said Brook. 'Well done!'

Eight

Next morning, Tilly woke early with butterflies in her stomach. Her mum dropped her at the World Horse Welfare Offices, where she met Laura.

'Hi, Tilly. Thank you so much for doing this,' she said.

'Thank *you*,' said Tilly. 'I can't believe I'm going to Badminton!'

'You're more than just going. You're working there. You're part of it. World Horse Welfare is Badminton's nominated charity and it's a brilliant fundraiser for us. You'll be helping on the stand, selling prize draw tickets and merchandise. Here. Wear this.'

Laura handed Tilly a navy World Horse Welfare polo shirt. Tilly pulled it on over her vest top and as she looked down at the logo, she felt very proud. It was true what Laura had said, she did feel like part of the World Horse Welfare Badminton team. The minibus pulled away and Tilly sat back, her head filled with thoughts of what the day would be like.

After a long drive, they finally approached Badminton House. Tilly was excited about getting inside the grounds. The cross-country wouldn't be starting until 11 o'clock, but there was already a long queue. Laura and Tilly followed a procession of cars up the long driveway to the car park.

Badminton House was the biggest, grandest place Tilly had ever seen. She tried to imagine what it would be like living there, having hundreds of rooms to wander in and out of, and acres and acres of land.

'If I ever get to live in a stately home,' she told Laura, 'I'll definitely organise a three-day-event in my back garden!'

Once they'd parked, they made their way to the shopping village. Tilly's eyes bulged as she spotted all her favourite horse gear and clothing brands had stands. Everywhere she looked she could see things she wanted: new jodhpurs, leather

riding gloves, and every style of riding
boot. There were also lots of lovely things
for horses: snuggly fleece blankets, smart
leather bridles and luxury saddles. As well
as the riding and outdoor brands, there
were stands selling toys, jewellery, food,
drink, and even an art gallery.

'Some people don't come to Badminton
for the horses at all,' said Laura. 'They
come for the shopping and the champagne!
Cross-country day always
attracts the biggest
crowd, so hopefully
we'll have lots of
people visiting our
stand.'

The girls from
the fundraising team
and the volunteers
all wore World Horse
Welfare polo shirts,
which looked very
smart. As soon as
the stand was open,

the first crowds came to browse.

Tilly had a busy morning. She sold lots of t-shirts, riding gloves and coffee mugs. She handed out leaflets about the rehab centres and horse loan scheme and encouraged people to sign up and add their names to an anti-cruelty petition. Occasionally people asked her advice about looking after their horses. This made her feel very important.

World Horse Welfare

One woman wanted to know if it was okay for her daughter to feed her pony little and often, and then the woman went on to explain that 'little' was a whole bucket and 'often' meant four times a day. Tilly knew the answer immediately. Overfeeding could be as cruel and as harmful as underfeeding. She'd had to deal with a similar thing when Cynthia and Parkview Pickle had first joined Silver Shoe. Too much food had made Pickle overweight and difficult to manage. As soon as she'd started eating a healthy balanced diet, her physique and behaviour had improved.

Another woman asked about how she could protect her horse from thieves. Again, Tilly remembered her own experience, when Magic was nearly stolen. He'd been mistaken for the Derby winner, Moonshadow, who was staying at Silver Shoe. Luckily Tilly and Mia had been close by and managed to stop the thieves getting away. Tilly explained that keeping a horse in a secure environment was very important, as well as getting it micro-chipped.

'Well done, Tilly,' said Laura. 'You're doing brilliantly. For someone so young, you know loads about horses. You should get a job on our advice line!'

Tilly grinned.

'Do you fancy some lunch? Let's get something to eat, then we can take a couple of the collection buckets over to the cross-country course. That will give you a chance to see some of the action.'

They bought delicious filled bagels for lunch and fresh orange juice. They sat down in the main arena and watched as they munched. A horse was getting skittish as it waited to start its round.

'I hope he calms down,' said Tilly.

'I expect he will once he gets going. At a competition like this, there's so much tension in the air. The horses can sense it too. They're anticipating the excitement to come.'

When they'd finished eating, Laura fetched two buckets and suggested going over to the lake where they could watch the riding and collect money from spectators.

'It's always dramatic near there,' Laura explained. 'Especially when the riders end up taking a swim!'

They made their way through the crowds. Tilly's heart was beating fast with the thrill of it all.

Nine

Tilly followed Laura through the deer park. She didn't need to shake her bucket much. People just kept stopping her and putting coins in. Whenever a horse and rider went by, everyone cheered. Tilly tried to see if she could recognise who they were, but they were always going too fast.

When they reached the lake, she could see why Laura had chosen it as a good spot. They arrived just as one of the horses came galloping by, hooves thundering.

The rider, wearing a bright red polo shirt
and grey helmet, dipped low as the horse's
front
legs rose up. They cleared the fence and
came crashing into the water. There was
an incredible splash.

'I'd love to do that one day,' whispered
Tilly.

'Maybe you will,' said Laura. 'With
the horse you were telling me about –
your rescue horse. What's his name?'

'Magic Spirit,' said Tilly, wondering what Magic would make of it all.

'That would make a great story for World Horse Welfare: Rescue Horse wins Badminton!'

'I wish,' said Tilly.

'You never know,' said Laura.

The crowd began to cheer and yell again, as the next horse came towards the lake. Tilly recognised the purple shirt and helmet of the rider and her beautiful chestnut mare. She'd seen her on television before. It was so exciting to think she was only a few feet away from a top eventer.

They made the jump, but landed heavily and the rider lost her balance. Her foot came free from the stirrup and she wobbled sideways. Everyone gasped as it looked as though she was about to fall into the water. But somehow she managed to steady herself, and moments later she was sitting up straight, feet in position, ready to carry on competing.

'Phew!' said Laura. 'I thought that was it for her!'

'Me too,' said Tilly. 'I can't believe she got back on track. What a rider!'

'I expect they'll show that bit on television. We should get back to the stand, give the girls a hand for the last hour.'

'Okay,' said Tilly. The day had gone so quickly, she couldn't believe it was almost over. She gave the lake one last glance then followed Laura through the crowds.

The last hour was very busy. There seemed to be an endless queue of people keen to sign the petition or ask for advice. Tilly managed to sell more than a dozen World Horse Welfare t-shirts, then eventually it was time to pack up. Just as they were starting to put things away, another customer came over and began browsing the books. Tilly looked up.

It was Tina Ford, one of her eventing heroines.

'C-can I help you?' she whispered, star-struck.

'Oh, hi,' said Tina. 'I'm just looking. I wanted to make sure I got to the World Horse Welfare stand before it closed. I really support the work you do. It's great!'

'Thanks,' said Tilly. She tried to stop herself, but it was hard to not stare at Tina. As she stared she felt as though she knew her – from all the eventing she'd watched on TV.

'I – I'm really impressed by you too,' she croaked. 'Is there any chance you could, er, give me your autograph?'

'Sure,' said Tina. Tilly didn't have anything for Tina to write on, then she noticed a marker pen that had been used for labelling boxes and a World Horse Welfare leaflet lying nearby. She grabbed them.

'You can write on this,' she said.

'Who do I make it out to?'

'I'm Tilly. Tilly Redbrow.'

Tina took the pen and wrote, 'To Tilly, Keep up the good work! Love Tina Ford.'

'Thanks,' said Tilly, barely able to contain her excitement. She couldn't wait to show Mia, Cally and Brook.

When Tina Ford left the stand, Tilly turned to Laura and grinned.

'Did you see? Did you see who that was?'

'I certainly did. She's a big supporter of World Horse Welfare. I'm pleased you got to meet her. Give me a hand with these boxes, will you? We can load them into the back of the bus.'

Tilly and Laura took a couple of boxes each and carried them out to the car park.

On the way, Laura's phone began to ring. She stopped, put her boxes down, and answered it. Tilly sat and waited. The way Laura was pacing, it seemed as though it was an important call. She was smiling so it looked like good news.

When she'd finished she came over to Tilly. She was still smiling.

'Well, after a really great day, there's some more lovely news.'

'What is it?' asked Tilly.

'We've just had confirmation that Goliath is going to be moved, as soon as he's fit enough, to Knightsbridge, where he'll be assessed, and then hopefully trained as a drum horse for the Household Cavalry.'

'Wow!'

'It's a very prestigious role. Drum horses go on parade in public and they're well-known throughout the world. Goliath's got just the right build and temperament to do it. These horses need to be calm and solid. They have to stand very still and put up with flashing lights and loud noise, as well as holding the weight of those huge drums and a rider in full ceremonial uniform.'

'That's brilliant. I'm so pleased for him,' said Tilly, her mind full of images of Goliath looking proud and spectacular.

'Me too,' said Laura. 'We'll have to go and visit him when he's settled in.'

Tilly couldn't wait. Goliath was going to be owned by Her Majesty the Queen!

Ten

It was nearly six weeks before Laura
called Tilly and offered to take her to
Knightsbridge. When the day finally came,
Tilly was very excited, not just about
seeing Goliath, but about spending time
with Laura again. She really admired her.

Laura picked Tilly up from her house.

'It's quite a drive, but don't worry,'
said Laura. 'I've got lots of good music.
Do you like Country Rock?'

'Hmm.' Tilly pulled a face.

'Maybe we'll stick with the radio then. Okay, London, here we come! Have you ever been before?'

'A few times. I went to the Olympia Horse Show one Christmas.'

'Ah, we always have a stand there. Did you enjoy it?'

'It was brilliant. I won a backstage tour and met an incredible show jumper called Samson.'

'I think I remember him. Didn't he win the Puissance? With a French rider?'

'That's the one,' said Tilly. 'I helped calm him down just before the competition. I wasn't supposed to be in the stables, I lost my tour group and got into a bit of trouble – but it was worth it.'

Laura glanced at her as though she wasn't quite sure if she believed her. Then she smiled.

'You do get up to some amazing things, Tilly! If it was anyone else, I'd probably think they were lying, but you're different. You've got more horse sense than most people twice your age and with twice your experience.'

After a few hours on the motorway, the scenery began to change. The traffic built up and the buildings became taller and closer together. They were in London. The area called Knightsbridge was very grand. They even drove past Buckingham Palace. Eventually they pulled up alongside a beautiful old brick building.

'Well, here we are. The Household Cavalry Mounted Regiment Barracks.'

'So this is Goliath's new home,' said Tilly. 'It's so posh!'

'From rags to riches, eh? He'll be mixing with some of the most elite military groups. They look after the Queen!'

'Let's go find him,' said Tilly.

Laura and Tilly were led through a large yard to a stable block. The smell of hay and manure was reassuringly familiar, as was the sound of hooves on the ground.

'Your horse has settled in well,' said the officer who'd met them. 'We think he'll make a great addition to the regiment. The training will be intense. It takes over eighteen months to fully train a drum horse and not all of them make the grade. But we've got faith in Goliath. We'll do everything we can to get him through.'

Suddenly, Goliath's face appeared over the top of a stable door. He saw Tilly and Laura walking towards him and his ears pricked up.

'He recognises us,' said Tilly.

'I'm sure he does,' said the officer. 'After all, you saved his life!'

Tilly ran towards him. He nuzzled her shoulder for a moment. She let him nibble and nudge her bracelets, and as he did, she stroked his nose. She couldn't believe how well he looked. His eyes were bright and his whole body had filled out. His coat was free from rain scald and he looked expertly groomed.

'Can I go in?' said Tilly.

'Better still,' said the officer, 'we'll bring him out. He's going for a training session in a bit. You can stay and watch if you like.'

'Great.'

Tilly led Goliath out of his stable. She felt honoured. It was so different to the time he'd followed her out of that dilapidated barn. She'd felt sad then. Now she felt nothing but joy.

While Goliath waited to join his training session, Tilly stood with him. She stroked his back and ran her hand down his neatly-combed tail. She managed to collect a few strands of his tail-hair.

'I think you'll do brilliantly here, Goliath,' she whispered.

Goliath stared down at her and gave a soft nicker.

His training session was all about building trust and confidence. He and a few other trainee horses had to wait in a line, while an officer flapped flags and ribbons. In the background, crowd noise was played through a stereo. Tilly and Laura watched, fascinated. Two of the horses side-stepped when the flags brushed over their noses, and obviously they were a little agitated, but Goliath stood perfectly still.

'That's our boy!' said Laura proudly.

When the session was over, Laura talked to the officers about Goliath's progress. Tilly sat quietly, looking at Goliath, and pulled the strands of his tail-hair from her pocket.

When it was time to leave, Tilly was sorry to say goodbye.

'Be good,' she said, as she stroked Goliath's shoulder (which was as high as she could reach!). 'We'll come and see you again. And who knows, maybe one day we'll see you in a parade on TV!'

He lowered his head, so she kissed his nose and walked away. Laura caught up with Tilly at the car. She looked a little sad.

'It's lovely to see one of our horses achieve so much!' she said. 'It's funny but it never gets any easier – it's always hard to say goodbye.'

'I understand,' said Tilly.

'He's done so well,' said Laura, as she opened the car door. 'Of course, you played a big part in helping us rescue him, so you should be proud of yourself. You helped change the course of a horse's life.'

'I guess I did,' said Tilly. 'And I'd do it a million times over.'

'I knew you'd say that. You know, when you finish school, I think there's definitely an opportunity for you at World Horse Welfare.'

'That would be great!'

Tilly sighed with happiness. 'Before we go,' she added, 'I want to give you this.'

She handed Laura the bracelet she'd made from Goliath's tail-hairs.

'Oh!' said Laura. 'Thank you!'

'So you'll always feel close to him, no matter how far away he is.'

Laura tied the bracelet round her wrist and gave Tilly a big hug.

As they got into the car, Tilly thought of Magic – her own amazing rescue horse. She wished she could just press a button and be there with him, but with the long drive back to North Cosford she knew that wasn't going to happen.

She sat back, closed her eyes and day-dreamed about him instead. She imagined them leaping through the lake at Badminton together. Tilly knew Magic

was destined to be a winner with her as his rider. If Goliath could make it as a drum horse working for Her Majesty the Queen, then who knew what Magic might achieve one day?

Pippa's Top Tips

Make sure you regularly check the fencing around your pony's field. It should be secure so your pony and any other horses in the field can't escape, and it should be safe so they won't injure themselves.

Look out for the yellow plant, Ragwort. It often grows in well-grazed fields. It is poisonous to horses and must be pulled up from the roots.

If you suspect a horse or pony is being neglected or cruelly treated in any way, report it to World Horse Welfare.

If a horse is nervous or unsettled, approach calmly and quietly at a side angle, because an approach from the front might be intimidating.

How much feed you give your pony should be judged according to the work he's doing, the weather conditions, and how much grass he has.

If you're ever unsure about how much your pony should eat, ask someone experienced, or call one of the feed companies who will be able to advise you.

Always get help if you are having problems loading your horse or pony into a trailer. Often you'll be able to tempt him with some food in a bucket.

Never stand directly behind a horse that doesn't load into a trailer.

If your pony is turned out with other horses in the field, make sure he is regularly wormed. Horses and ponies need worming approximately three times a year, and they shouldn't be wormed by the same wormer each time.

Always watch your feet when you're around larger horses. You won't have any toes left if a shire horse steps on them!

Glossary

World Horse Welfare (p.9) – A charity dedicated to giving abused and neglected horses a second chance in life by rescuing and re-homing them. In the UK, World Horse Welfare have four farms open to visitors where many of their 2,000 horses are kept. Visit www.worldhorsewelfare.org for more information.

Badminton Horse Trials (p.18) – A world class three day event comprising dressage, cross-country and show jumping, which takes place at the end of April or beginning of May each year in the park of Badminton House, Gloucestershire.

Gelding (p.25) – A male horse that has been 'gelded' or had his testicles removed so that he is unable to reproduce.

hh / hands high (p.36) – Horses and ponies are measured in 'hands', a hand is 4 inches or 10.16 cm.

Skewbald (p.41) – A skewbald horse has a coat made up of white patches on a non-black base coat, such as chestnut or bay.

Head collar/halter (p.42) – This is used to lead a horse or pony, or tie it up, and usually made of leather or webbing.

Draught horse (p.43) – A large horse bred for hard, heavy tasks such as ploughing and farm labour. Draught horses tend to be strong and patient with a docile temperament.

Farrier (p.53) – Also known as a blacksmith. A specialist who takes care of horses' hooves, including hoof trimming and shoeing.

Grooming (p.54) – Regular grooming cleans your horse and will prevent any chafing under tack. It keeps your horse healthy and comfortable and will help you form a relationship with him.

Star and snip (p.61) – These are common facial markings: a 'star' is a white marking between or above the eyes, and a 'snip' is a white marking on the muzzle, between the nostrils.

Cross country (p.66) – A test of the boldness, speed, endurance and jumping ability for horse and rider as they negotiate fixed natural obstacles like logs, ditches, streams, banks and fences.

Rain scald (p.89) – A common skin disease in horses, caused by a bacterial infection that gets into the skin. It can occur when horses are exposed to wet weather and muddy conditions for long periods of time. It is not infectious.

Points of a Horse

1. poll
2. ear
3. eye
4. mane
5. crest
6. withers
7. back
8. loins
9. croup
10. dock
11. flank
12. tail
13. tendons
14. hock joint
15. stomach
16. elbow
17. heel
18. hoof
19. coronet band
20. pastern
21. fetlock joint
22. cannon bone
23. knee
24. shoulder
25. chin groove
26. nostril
27. muzzle
28. nose
29. cheekbone
30. forelock

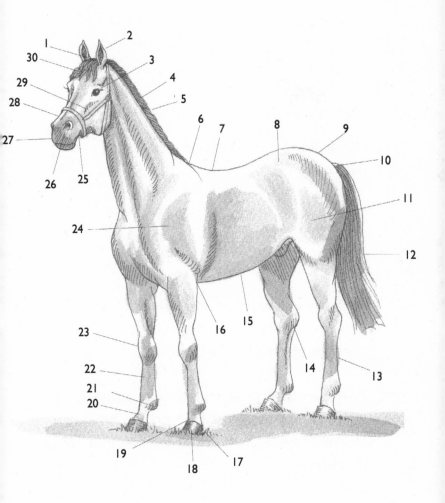

Pippa Funnell

"Winning is amazing for a minute, but then I am striving again to reach my next goal."

I began learning to ride when I was six, on a little pony called Pepsi.

When I was seven, I joined my local Pony Club – the perfect place to learn more about riding and caring for horses.

By the time I was fourteen and riding my first horse, Sir Barnaby, my dream of being an event rider was starting to take shape.

Two years later, I was offered the opportunity to train as a working pupil in Norfolk with Ruth McMullen, the legendary riding teacher. I jumped at the chance.

In 1987, Sir Barnaby and I won the individual gold together at the Young Rider European Championships, which was held in Poland.

Since then, hard work and determination have taken me all the way to the biggest eventing competitions in the world. I've been lucky and had success at major events like Bramham, Burghley, Badminton, Luhmühlen, Le Lion d'Angers, Hickstead, Blenheim, Windsor, Saumur, Pau, Kentucky – and the list goes on…

I married William Funnell in 1993. William is an international show jumper and horse breeder. He has helped me enormously with my show jumping. We live on a farm in the beautiful Surrey countryside – with lots of stables!

Every sportsman or woman's wildest dream is to be asked to represent their country at the Olympics. So in 2000, when I was chosen for the Sydney Olympics, I was delighted. It was even more special to be part of the silver medal winning team.

Then, in 2003, I became the first (and only) person to win eventing's most coveted prize – the Rolex Grand Slam. The Grand Slam (winning three of the big events in a row – Badminton, Kentucky and Burghley) is the only three-day eventing slam in the sporting world.

2004 saw another Olympics and another call-up. Team GB performed brilliantly again and won another well-deserved silver medal, and I was lucky enough to win an individual bronze.

Having had several years without any top horses, I spent my time producing youngsters, so it was great in 2010 when one of those came through – Redesigned, a handsome chestnut gelding. In June that year I won my third Bramham International Horse Trials title on Redesigned. We even managed a clear show jumping round in the pouring rain! By the end of 2010, Redesigned was on the squad for the World Championships in Kentucky where we finished fifth.

Today, as well as a hectic competition schedule, I'm also busy training horses for the future. At the Billy Stud, I work with my husband, William, and top breeder, Donal Barnwell, to produce top-class sport horses.

And in between all that I love writing the *Tilly's Pony Tails* books, and I'm also a trustee of World Horse Welfare, a fantastic charity dedicated to giving abused and neglected horses a second chance in life. For more information, visit their website at www.worldhorsewelfare.org.

Acknowledgements

Three years ago when my autobiography was
published I never imagined that I would find myself
writing children's books. Huge thanks go to Louisa
Leaman for helping me to bring Tilly to life, and
to Jennifer Miles for her wonderful illustrations.

Many thanks to Fiona Kennedy for persuading and
encouraging me to search my imagination and for all her
hard work, along with the rest of the team at Orion.
Due to my riding commitments I am not the easiest
person to get hold of as my agent Jonathan Marks
at MTC has found. It's a relief he has been able
to work on all the agreements for me.

Much of my thinking about Tilly has been done
out loud in front of family, friends and godchildren –
thank you all for listening.

More than anything I have to acknowledge my four-legged
friends – my horses. It is thanks to them, and the
great moments I have had with them, that I was able to
create a girl, Tilly, who like me follows her passions.

Pippa Funnell
Forest Green, February 2009

For more about Tilly and
Silver Shoe Farm – including pony tips,
quizzes and everything you ever wanted
to know about horses –
visit www.tillysponytails.co.uk